W9-BML-695

For my father. Thank you. —M. S.
For Cynthia. —A. J.

First published in the United States in 2004 by Chronicle Books LLC.

Illustrations © 2004 by Alison Jay.
Text and design copyright © 2004 by The Templar Company plc.
Originally published in the United Kingdom in 2004 by Templar Publishing.
All rights reserved.

Book design by Janie Louise Hunt.
Typeset in Garton.
The illustrations in this book were rendered
in Alkyd paint with crackle-glaze varnish.
Manufactured in China.

Library of Congress Cataloging-in-Publication Data available.

Distributed in Canada by Raincoast Books
9050 Shaughnessy Street, Vancouver,
British Columbia V6P 6E5

10 9 8 7 6 5 4 3 2 1

Chronicle Books LLC
85 Second Street, San Francisco,
California 94105

www.chroniclekids.com

The Emperor's New Clothes

Retold by Marcus Sedgwick * Illustrated by Alison Jay

chronicle books · san francisco

MCL FOR
NEPTUNE CITY
PUBLIC LIBRARY

ONE DAY the emperor got out of bed
and slowly scratched his sleepy head.

Another royal day had dawned,
but he had nothing to put on.
Of all his crowns and robes and stuff,
no outfit seemed quite grand enough.

"What I need, I do declare,
is a brand new suit of clothes to wear.
Clothes to make my people see
what a fine king they have in me!"

Before he could utter one word more,
a knock came at the palace door.
There stood two weasels, looking pleased.
"We have just what the emperor needs!"

"We're the finest tailors in the land!
We can weave you clothes so grand
your subjects will cry, 'Goodness me!
There is no emperor
quite like he!'"

"THAT'S WHAT I WANT!
THAT'S JUST THE THING!"
exclaimed the vain
and conceited king.

"AND THAT'S NOT ALL," the tailors said,
"for we weave spells as well as thread.
All who dull or foolish be,
our magic clothes they cannot see!

A bit more gold
will buy this spell.
We're sure that it will
serve you well!"

THE KING WAS DELIGHTED.

"Start straight away!
Arrange a grand procession day!
I'll wear the clothes which you have made.
My subjects will cheer as I parade!"

"But can we afford it?" the treasurer cried,
opening the lid of the treasury wide.
The chamberlain agreed, "We've spent too much
on trousers, shirts, and hats and such!"

"NONSENSE! This suit will let me see
those who wise or foolish be—
those unfit for the office they hold!
Hare and Tortoise, do as you're told!"

But the emperor had made an awful mistake.
The weasels weren't tailors, they were FAKE.
And when Hare left them to start their work,
the two young rascals began to smirk.

Smiling and joking, giggling and more,
they laughed and rolled upon the floor.
"I never imagined we'd fool them so well."
"Who would have thought
they'd believe in a spell!"

"How easily people are taken in,
even by a tale so very thin!"
"But the story's a good one, woven with care.
And one that was told with a
great deal of flair!"

Peeking in through
the crack in the door,
Hare wondered what all
the laughter was for.

Many days passed, without a sign
of any clothes, either shabby or fine.
The poor old emperor began to doubt
that he'd ever get his parade shoes out!

"It's time I saw these wonderful clothes,"
moaned the emperor,
grumpily scratching his nose.
"But suppose, when I visit, I can't see a thing.
Then I'd look like a fool
and I am the KING!
I don't want to seem like a dunderhead!
I'll send my servants to look instead!"

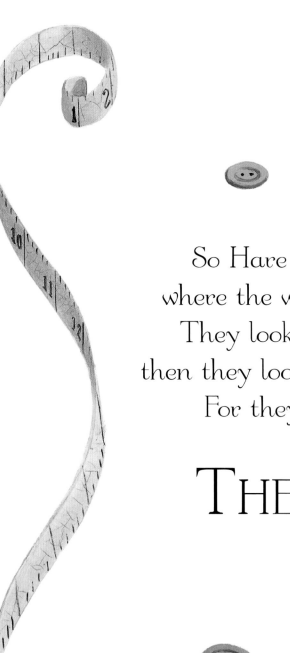

So Hare and Tortoise went down to the room
where the weasels pretended to work on their loom.
They looked for the suit that was waiting below,
then they looked at each other and thought, "Oh NO!"
For they couldn't see anything there at all!
What to tell the emperor?
THEY HAD TO STALL!

By now the emperor was eager to know
what had become of his fabulous clothes.
"Tell me!" he cried to Tortoise and Hare,
of the clothes they'd not seen,
the clothes that weren't there.

"What are they like? Are they sumptuous and rich?
Are they special and lovely and beautifully stitched?"

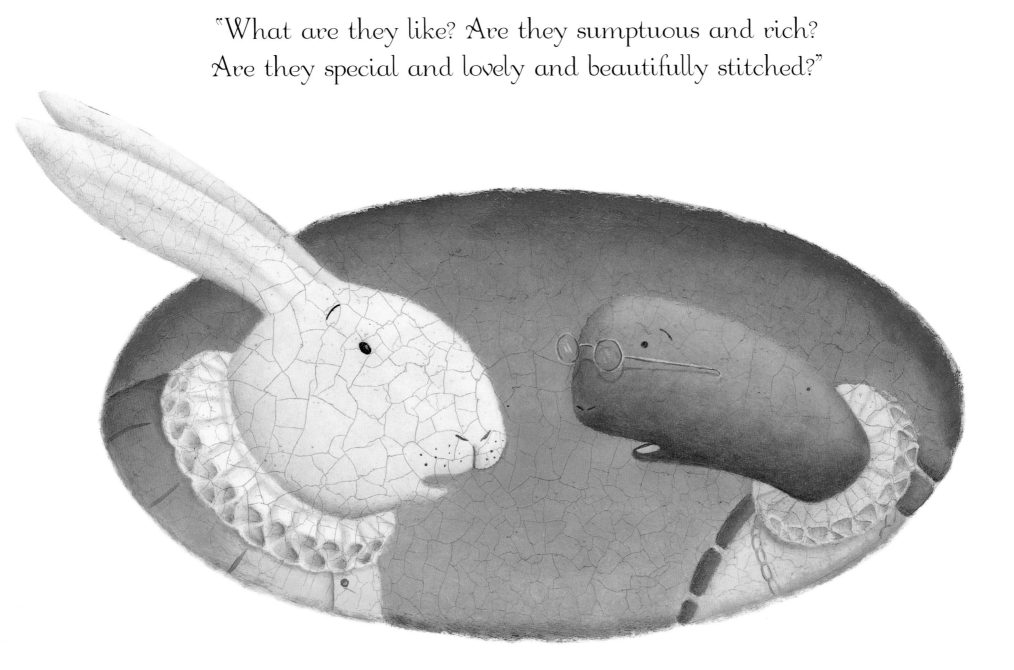

Hare and Tortoise wished for somewhere to hide.
"They look wonderful, Majesty!" both of them lied.

The day of the procession
at last had come,
eagerly awaited by everyone.
The weasels fussed
and patted and preened.
Slyly, they told him,
"They fit like a dream!"
And the emperor pretended not to care
that he seemed to be
dressed in clothes THAT
WEREN'T THERE.

As the procession set out,
everyone stared and gawked,
too frightened to say what they
really thought.

But then came a voice, a small frog's call,
"LOOK! The emperor's wearing **nothing** at all!"

He didn't understand why they were so impressed,
when the foolish old lion wasn't properly dressed.
After that, the secret was out,
and everyone started to point and shout.
Laughter rang out. What a hullabaloo!

For the trick was EXPOSED,
and THE EMPEROR, TOO!